PICTURE BOOK STUDIO

Hans Christian Andersen
Lisbeth Zwerger

THE NIGHTINGALE

Translation by Anthea Bell

In China, as you know, the Emperor is Chinese, and so are all his people. The Emperor had the most magnificent palace in the world, made all of fine porcelain. Out in the garden grew wonderfully beautiful flowers, and the loveliest of all had little silver bells tied to them that rang as you went by, so that you couldn't fail to notice them. Beyond the garden was a very beautiful wood that went all the way down to the deep blue sea. Great ships could sail right in under its branches, and in the branches, there lived a nightingale who sang so sweetly that even the poor fisherman, busy each night with his nets, would stop and listen to its song. "Dear God, how beautiful it is!" he said. Then he went to work, and forgot the bird, but the next night when the nightingale sang again, he said the same: "Dear God, how beautiful it is!"

Travelers came from far off lands and marvelled at the city and the palace and the garden, but when they heard the nightingale every one of them said, "Ah, that's the best thing of all!"

And the travelers went home, and learned men wrote books about the palace and the garden, and they praised the nightingale most of all. The books went all over the world, and at last they came to the Emperor too. He read and read, delighted with the wonderful descriptions. And then he read: "But the nightingale is best of all."

"What's all this?" said the Emperor. "Nightingale? I never heard of it!" And he summoned his Lord in Waiting.

"They say a remarkable bird called the nightingale is the finest thing in all my Empire. Why has nobody told me about this bird?"

"I never heard of it," said the Lord in Waiting.

"I want it to come and sing for me this evening," said the Emperor. "It seems all the world knows what I have here, except me!"

"I never heard of it myself," repeated the Lord in Waiting. "But I'll look for it, and I'll find it."

The Lord in Waiting ran all through the palace and no one had ever heard of the nightingale. So the Lord in Waiting went back to the Emperor and said, "Your Majesty mustn't believe everything he reads in books."

"But the book was sent by the high and mighty Emperor of Japan, so it must be true. I want to hear the nightingale!"

"Tsing-pe!" said the Lord in Waiting, and he ran off again, and half the Court followed him. At last they found a poor little kitchen girl, who said, "The nightingale? Oh, yes! My poor sick mother lives down by the shore. When I return from a visit, I stop for a rest in the wood and I hear the nightingale sing. It brings tears to my eyes, as if my mother were kissing me."

"Little kitchenmaid," said the Lord in Waiting, "I will get you a steady job here in the kitchen and permission to watch the Emperor eat his dinner if you can take us to the nightingale, for it is summoned to Court this evening."

So they went out to the wood. And as they were going a cow began to moo. "We've found the nightingale!"

"No, those are cows," said the kitchenmaid.

Then they heard frogs croaking. "Exquisite!"

"No, those are frogs," said the kitchenmaid. And then the nightingale began to sing.

"There it is!" said the little girl. "Listen, listen!" And she pointed up to a small gray bird.

"Little nightingale," called the kitchenmaid, "our Emperor wants you to sing for him."

"He's very welcome," said the nightingale, and it sang very beautifully, for it thought the Emperor himself was present.

"My dear, good little nightingale," said the Lord in Waiting. "You are invited to a party at Court this evening, where you will delight his Imperial Majesty with your lovely song."

"It sounds best out here in the green woods," said the nightingale, but it went along with them, on hearing it was the Emperor's wish.

What a cleaning and a polishing there was at the palace! In the middle of the great hall they placed a golden perch for the nightingale. The entire Court was there, gazing at the little gray bird. The Emperor nodded to it and the nightingale sang so sweetly that tears rose to the Emperor's eyes and flowed down his cheeks, and then the nightingale sang yet more beautifully, so that its song went right to the heart. The Emperor was so delighted that he said the nightingale was to have his own golden slipper to wear around its neck. But the nightingale thanked him and said it already had its reward. "I have seen tears in the eyes of the Emperor, and what more could I wish for?"

The nightingale was a great success. And now it was to stay at Court, and have its own cage, and be allowed out twice by day and once by night. Twelve menservants were to go with it, each holding tight to a silken ribbon tied to the bird's leg. Of course, going out like that was no pleasure at all.

One day a big parcel came for the Emperor, with Nightingale written on it. "Here's a new book about our famous bird," said the Emperor. But it was a little wind-up toy, an artificial nightingale, covered all over with diamonds and rubies and sapphires. It sang one of the real nightingale's songs, and its tail went up and down, all shining with silver and gold. It had a little ribbon around its neck with the words: The Emperor of Japan's nightingale is a poor thing beside the nightingale of the Emperor of China.

"Now they can sing together!" said the Court. And sing they did, but it wasn't quite right.

So the artificial bird was to sing alone. It was just as great a success as the real bird, and it glittered like jewelry. It sang the same song thirty-three times, and still it wasn't tired. The Court would happily have heard the song again, but the Emperor thought it was time for the real nightingale to sing. But where had it gone? It had flown out of the open window, out and away, back to its own green wood.

"What's all this?" said the Emperor, and all the courtiers said the nightingale was a most ungrateful creature. "But we still have the better bird," they said, and the mechanical nightingale had to sing the same song again, for the thirty-fourth time. The Master of the Music praised the bird to the skies, and actually stated that it was better than the real nightingale, not just because of its plumage, glittering with so many lovely diamonds, but inside too. And the Master of the Music got permission to show the bird to all the people next Sunday, for the Emperor said they should hear it too. And hear it they did, and they were as happy as if they had gotten tipsy on tea, for tea is what the Chinese drink; and they all said Ooh! and pointed their fingers in the air, and nodded. However the poor fisherman who used to listen to the real nightingale said, "It sounds nice enough, and quite like the real bird, but there's something missing, I don't know what." And the real nightingale was banished from the Emperor's domains.

The artificial bird had a place on a silk cushion next to the Emperor's bed. And the Master of the Music wrote a book, in twenty-five volumes, about the mechanical bird, and all the people at Court pretended to have read it.

After a year the Emperor, the Court, and all the other Chinese now knew every little trill of the mechanical bird's song by heart, but they liked it all the better for that. One evening, however, as the artificial bird was singing its very best, and the Emperor lay in his bed listening, it went, "Twang!" and the wheels whirred around and the music stopped. So they fetched the watchmaker, and after much talk and much tinkering about with it, he got the bird to work again after a fashion. However, he said it mustn't be made to sing very often, because the little pegs on the cylinders had worn out and there was no way of replacing them without spoiling the tune. This was very sad indeed. They let the mechanical bird sing just once a year, and even that was a strain on it.

Five years passed by, and the Emperor was sick. He lay in his bed, cold and pale, next to the mechanical nightingale. The whole Court thought he was dead already, and went to pay their respects to the new Emperor. But the Emperor was not dead yet. The poor Emperor could hardly draw breath, and he felt as if something were sitting on his chest. He opened his eyes, and saw Death sitting there, wearing his own golden crown, and holding his own golden sabre in one hand and his banner in the other. And strange faces—some grim and hideous and others blessed and mild—peered out from among the hangings of the bed. They were the Emperor's good deeds and bad deeds, looking at him. "Remember this?" they whispered, and the sweat broke out on his forehead.

"No, no! Music!" he cried. "Music on the great Chinese drum, to keep me from hearing what you say!" But on they went, and Death kept nodding at everything they said. "Music, music!" cried the Emperor. "Sing, my little golden bird, oh, sing, sing for me now, sing!"

But the bird was silent. And Death gazed and gazed at the Emperor, and all was terribly still. At that moment the loveliest song came in through the window—the real nightingale, who had heard the Emperor was sick. Death listened and said, "Go on, go on!"

"Yes, if you give me that fine gold sabre! Yes, if you give me that banner! Yes, if you will give me the Emperor's crown!" So Death gave up each treasure for one of the nightingale's songs. The nightingale sang of the quiet graveyard. Then Death longed for his own garden, and drifted out of the window like cold white mist.

"Thank you, thank you, little bird" said the Emperor. "I know you now! I drove you away, yet you have driven Death from my heart. How can I reward you?"

"You have rewarded me already," said the nightingale. "I brought tears to your eyes the first time I sang to you. But you must sleep now, and be fresh and strong when you wake. Now I will sing for you." The nightingale sang, and the Emperor fell asleep into a sweet, gentle, and refreshing slumber.

The Emperor woke in the sunshine, feeling strong and healthy. He was alone, for all his servants thought he was dead, but the nightingale still sat there singing.

"You must stay with me forever," said the Emperor.

"I cannot live or nest in a palace; but let me come to you when I feel like it, and I'll sit on the branch outside your window and sing in the evening, to gladden your heart and fill it with thoughts. I will sing of those who are happy and those who are sad, I will sing of the bad and the good around you. But you must promise me one thing."

"Anything," said the Emperor, and he stood there in the imperial robes he had put on again, holding his heavy golden sabre to his breast.

"Please do not tell anyone you have a little bird who tells you everything; that will be best." Then the nightingale flew away.

The Emperor's servants came in to look at him lying dead, and they stood there amazed.

"Good morning," said the Emperor.

A Michael Neugebauer Book
Copyright © 1984 by Neugebauer Press, Salzburg.
Published by Picture Book Studio, Saxonville, MA.
Distributed in the United States by Simon & Schuster.
Distributed in Canada by Vanwell Publishing, St. Catharines, Ontario.
All rights reserved. Printed in Hong Kong.
10 9 8 7 6 5 4 3 2 1

Library of Congress Cataloging-in-Publication Data
Andersen, H.C. (Hans Christian), 1805-1875.
[Nattergalen. English]
The nightingale / written by H.C. Andersen; illustrated by Lisbeth Zwerger; translated by Anthea Bell.
p. cm. —(Pixies; #22)
Summary: Though the emperor banishes the nightingale in preference for a jeweled mechanical imitation, the little bird remains faithful and returns years later when the emperor is near death and no one else can help him.
ISBN 0-88708-269-6: $4.95
[1. Fairy tales. 2. Nightingales—Fiction.] I. Bell, Anthea.
II. Zwerger, Lisbeth, ill. III. Title. IV. Series.
PZ8. A542Ni   1993
[Fic]—dc20   92-33813
CIP
AC